FUTURISTIC ELECTRIC Airplanes

Kerrily Sapet

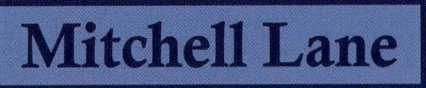

PUBLISHERS

2001 SW 31st Avenue
Hallandale, FL 33009
www.mitchelllane.com

Copyright © 2020 by Mitchell Lane Publishers. All rights reserved. No part of this book may be reproduced without written permission from the publisher. Printed and bound in the United States of America.

Library of Congress Cataloging-in-Publication Data
Names: Sapet, Kerrily, 1972- author.
Title: Futuristic electric airplanes / by Kerrily Sapet.Description: First edition. | Hallandale, FL : Mitchell Lane Publishers, 2020. | Series: Futuristic electric vehicles | Includes bibliographical references and index.
Identifiers: LCCN 2018028578| ISBN 9781680203462 (library bound) | ISBN 9781680203479 (ebook)
Subjects: LCSH: Electric airplanes—Juvenile literature. | Aeronautics—Environmental aspects— Juvenile literature.
Classification: LCC TL683.3 .S36 2020 | DDC 629.133/34—dc23
LC record available at https://lccn.loc.gov/2018028578

First Edition, 2020.
Author: Kerrily Sapet
Designer: Ed Morgan
Editor: Sharon F. Doorasamy

Series: Futuristic Electric
Title: Airplanes / by Kerrily Sapet

Hallandale, FL : Mitchell Lane Publishers, [2020]

Library bound ISBN: 9781680203462
eBook ISBN: 9781680203479

PHOTO CREDITS: Design Elements, freepik.com, Cover Photo: NASA, p. 5 LOC, p. 6 freepik.com, p. 7 @flaticon, p. 9 VCG/VCG via Getty Images, p. 11 NASA, p. 13 Mustafa Yalcin/Anadolu Agency/Getty Images, p. 15 NASA, p. 16 NASA, p. 17 Ironie/Wikicommons CC-BY-SA-2.5, p. 18 PLANETAIRE/Wikicommons Copyrighted free use, p. 19 Freepik.com, p. 22 Freepik.com, p. 25 NASA, p. 27 Jean Revillard/Solar Impulse2 via Getty Images, p. 28-29 freepik.com

CONTENTS

Chapter One
A "WHOPPER FLYING MACHINE" — 4

Chapter Two
AIRPLANES GO GREEN — 8

Chapter Three
UP, UP AND AWAY — 14

Chapter Four
AMAZING AIRCRAFT — 20

Chapter Five
THE FUTURE LOOKS ELECTRIC — 24

WHAT YOU SHOULD KNOW — 28
GLOSSARY — 29
WORKS CONSULTED — 30
FURTHER READING — 31
ON THE INTERNET — 31
INDEX — 32
ABOUT THE AUTHOR — 32

Words in **bold** throughout can be found in the Glossary.

Chapter One

A "WHOPPER FLYING MACHINE"

People have always dreamed of flying. In Greek mythology, the inventor Daedalus flew using wings made of wax, feathers, and thread. In the 1400s, artist Leonardo da Vinci sketched hundreds of pictures of flying machines. More than 400 years later, two brothers showed the world that human flight was no longer just a dream.

When Wilbur and Orville Wright were young boys in Ohio, their father bought them a wooden toy plane. A small propeller on the plane turned using twisted rubber bands. The boys played with the toy so much that they broke it. They built copies of it. They also made kites to sell to friends. Fascinated with the idea of flying, the Wrights spent years studying flight and making gliders. "Flight was generally looked upon as an impossibility," said Orville. The brothers added propellers and a gas engine to a large glider made of wood and fabric. Their nephew called it a "whopper flying machine."

On December 17, 1903, the Wrights tested their flying machine on the breezy sand dunes of Kitty Hawk, North Carolina. With Orville at the controls, the plane flew for 12 seconds before safely returning to the ground. "They done it! They done it!" shouted one observer. People could hardly believe it. A headline in a French newspaper read "Flyers or Liars?"

News of the first successful flight spread. Other inventors learned from the Wright brothers' designs and began to improve on them. The first flights were cold. There was no insulation from the air. They were also bumpy because pilots couldn't fly high enough to reach calmer air. World War I (1914–1918) and World War II (1939–1945) spurred further design and engineering advances. People started building heavier and bigger airplanes with more impressive engines and using stronger materials. People began to fly just for fun.

First successful flight of the Wright Flyer, by the Wright brothers in 1903

CHAPTER ONE

Today's airplanes use powerful jet engines. They fly higher, faster, and farther than ever. They carry billions of people to destinations around the globe. An average of 8 million people take flight every day. During busy travel times there may be as many as 16,000 planes in the skies at once. More air traffic means more noise pollution and more air pollution.

Airplanes burn billions of gallons of jet fuel each year. Jet fuel is made from petroleum. Petroleum is a **fossil fuel** formed underground over millions of years from the remains of plants and animals. Fossil fuels are **nonrenewable resources**. Once they're used, they're gone. Fossil fuels such as petroleum and coal are fast being depleted.

A "Whopper Flying Machine"

When fossil fuels are burned to release their energy, they emit carbon dioxide. Carbon dioxide is a colorless, odorless gas. Each gallon of burned jet fuel releases 21 pounds of carbon dioxide into the air. Carbon dioxide builds up in the **atmosphere**. This buildup causes the Earth's temperature to rise.

Airplanes release about 500 million tons of carbon dioxide into the atmosphere every year. The world needs a solution to airplane pollution. Powering airplanes with electricity, instead of jet fuel, could be the answer.

Fun Facts

1 A Boeing 737, an average size plane, burns about 12.5 gallons of fuel every minute.

2 The distance of the Wright brothers' first flight is shorter than the wingspan of most of today's commercial airplanes.

Chapter Two

AIRPLANES GO GREEN

The Wright brothers worked together to build the first airplane. Today, dozens of companies are teaming up to design and build electric airplanes. The electric motors powering their designs offer big advantages over fuel-burning engines. Electricity produces **zero emissions**. Zero emissions means it doesn't give off any pollution. Electric motors are powered by batteries that spin a propeller. Electric motors are smaller, quieter, and lighter. Jet engines need to suck in air to produce power. Electric motors don't need air. Motors can be mounted on planes in different ways and have fewer parts, making them easier to fix.

Building any new airplane design takes years of work. Experts draw detailed pictures of the plane. Next they make models. Then they test their models in wind tunnels to ensure that they are **aerodynamic**. Aerodynamic airplanes fly smoothly through the air. Computer simulations allow engineers to study how the plane would behave in different situations. Large airplanes can have more than a million parts. Each part is tested to make sure it doesn't fail.

Fun Fact

China, Norway, Germany, and Australia are among the countries developing electric airplanes.

China's first electric airplane, the RX1E, made a test flight on November 1, 2017. The two-seater has a two-hour flight range.

CHAPTER TWO

Designing an electric airplane isn't as easy as swapping a jet engine for an electric motor. There are challenges. The biggest problem is batteries. Electric motors run on batteries. Today's batteries can't match the turbo power of a jet engine. Batteries deliver far less energy per pound than jet fuel. A Boeing 787, a large commercial plane, holds 223,000 pounds of fuel. A battery with the same amount of energy would weigh 4.5 million pounds. Planes can't fly carrying that much weight.

The bigger the airplane, the more energy it takes to lift off and fly. So companies are starting small. They are designing electric airplanes to carry a few passengers and fly short routes. "You learn and you keep scaling up until you reach commercial airliner classes," says Andreas Klockner of the German Aerospace Center.

Some of the designs in progress look like today's airplanes. Others resemble flying cars or hovering drones.

> "Future electric aircraft will look nothing like the aircraft of today, and they will be able to fly with much less energy. We'll redesign aircraft around electric motors."
> —VENAK VISWANATHAN, BATTERY SCIENTIST, CARNEGIE MELLON UNIVERSITY

NASA is one of many groups around the world designing and testing electric airplanes. NASA's X-57 plane, nicknamed "Maxwell," features six motors on each wing and larger motors on each wingtip. Eviation, an electric airplane company, is building a plane with propellers on the wingtips and on the plane's tail.

Airplanes Go Green

NASA's X-57

NASA'S X-PLANES

Since 1958, NASA has pioneered aircraft technology with innovative X-planes. The first X-plane broke records for flying faster than the speed of sound. NASA's latest X-planes push green technology. "We need the X-planes to prove, in an undeniable way, how that tech can make aviation more Earth friendly," says Jaiwon Shin, associate administrator for NASA's Aeronautics Research Mission Directorate.

CHAPTER TWO

Innovative airline companies are partnering with small electric airplane companies such as Wright Electric and Zunum Aero (Zunum is Mayan for "hummingbird"). EasyJet, a large European airline, and Wright Electric are working to build an electric airplane. Wright Electric founder Jeffrey Engler says small companies could help move the massive aviation industry away from its reliance on jet fuel.

"If you're a mouse, you don't have a lot of control in the world. You're scurrying around trying not to get stepped on. But if you're a mouse in the right position, you could tickle the foot of an elephant to move it in the right direction."

—JEFFREY ENGLER, WRIGHT ELECTRIC

Airplanes Go Green

The Airbus E-Fan electric aircraft prepares for a flight during the international Paris Air Show in 2015. The E-Fan X will use a combination of jet and electric motors.

Airbus, an airplane manufacturer, has teamed up with Rolls Royce and Siemens. Together they are building a **hybrid** plane called "E-Fan X." E-Fan X will use a combination of jet engines and electric motors.

"For the first time in my career I can envisage a future without jet fuel," says Carolyn McCall of EasyJet. "It is now more a matter of when, not if, a short-haul electric plane will fly."

Chapter Three

UP, UP AND AWAY

For any airplane to fly, four **forces** need to be in balance. The four forces are lift, weight, thrust, and drag. Lift holds the airplane up in the air. Weight, caused by the pull of Earth's gravity, brings the airplane down. Thrust moves the airplane forward. A propeller or jet engine creates thrust by pulling in air and pushing it out in the opposite direction. Drag, caused by air rubbing against the airplane's surface, slows the plane down. The heavier the plane and the greater the drag, the more fuel or energy the plane uses.

An airplane's wings create lift because of the way the air moves over and under the wings. The size and shape of the wing affects the lift and drag. "A big wing turns into a whole lot of drag at fast speed," says Nick Borer of NASA. The experts designing NASA's X-57 have created a long, skinny lightweight wing to drag less through the air. They've also mounted motors on the wings to provide lift during takeoff. Engineers are researching different shapes for the plane's body. In one design, the airplane's wings are part of the body. This makes the airplane look like a large triangle.

An artist's concept of NASA's X-57 Maxwell, an all-electric experimental aircraft

CHAPTER THREE

Weight is critical for a machine that needs to lift off the ground and fly. A lighter plane takes less fuel to get airborne and fly. To cut down on weight, scientists are inventing new **composite** materials. Composite materials combine different materials to make stronger, lighter parts.

Batteries add extra weight to electric airplanes. The battery pack on NASA's X-57 plane weighs 850 pounds. Engineers are experimenting with new ways to attach the batteries on planes to help with the extra weight. Scientists are working to make batteries lighter and more powerful. This will increase the energy savings and flight range of airplanes. The batteries powering today's electric airplanes are rechargeable lithium-ion batteries. Lithium-ion batteries also power phones, laptops, and electric cars.

NASA's X-57 Battery System

Up, Up and Away

Fun Fact

Archaeologists believe ancient batteries may have been used in Iraq about 2000 years ago.

An artist's sketch of the Baghdad Battery, a clay jar reportedly unearthed near Baghdad in 1938. The jar contains an iron rod surrounded by a copper cylinder. Adding a solution like vinegar or lemon juice produces a small electric charge like that of a battery.

CHAPTER THREE

German glider pilot Klaus Ohlmann

Today's batteries allow for a plane to fly about 250 miles. Klaus Ohlmann piloted a record-setting electric airplane. He predicts that in five years batteries will have double that capacity and in 10 years, 10 times more **capacity**. Until then, scientists also are experimenting with fuel cells. Fuel cells combine hydrogen and oxygen to produce electricity.

Up, Up and Away

Several companies and universities are developing designs for electric planes. Teams are testing and improving their designs to maximize power, aerodynamics, energy efficiency, and safety. Most planes won't be in flight until 2020 at the earliest. Commercial electric airliners are still several years away. But recent technological advances make electric airplanes more of a possibility now than ever before.

Fun Fact

Before planes fly passengers, they must pass thousands of safety tests, from simulated lightning bolts to bird strikes.

Chapter Four

AMAZING AIRCRAFT

Most commercial passenger planes flying the skies today look similar. There is a rounded nose, tube-shaped body, wings, two engines, and a tail. The airplanes of tomorrow could look very different. Experts around the world are reimagining the airplane and testing electric airplane **prototypes**.

NASA's X-57 electric airplane, Maxwell, features 14 electric motors. "When you go from two to twelve to fourteen motors, there's a whole bunch of new stuff that as an aircraft designer you never really thought about before that you can start to think about," says NASA's Borer. Six small electric motors line Maxwell's long, sleek wings. A larger motor sits on each wingtip. All 14 motors power Maxwell's takeoff. The two larger motors take over during flight. Maxwell's massive battery pack fills up the backseat. On the ground, the batteries are charged using solar cells. Maxwell's first test flight is scheduled for 2018.

Eviation, a company based in Israel, is testing an electric airplane they call "Alice." Alice is designed for short trips between cities. The plane can carry nine passengers and two crew members with a range of up to 600 miles. "Almost no one is riding in forty-year old cars," says Eviation's founder Omer Bar-Yohay, "and yet most aircraft in our size category derive from designs that are at least four decades old." Alice has a propeller at the tail and two propellers at the wingtips. It runs on 6,000 pounds of batteries. Eviation aims for Alice to take flight by 2021.

Wright Electric is designing an electric 10-seat plane and working with EasyJet on a 150-seat plane for flights under 300 miles. That's the distance between New York and Boston. Wright Electric will mount the plane's batteries inside shipping containers so they can be easily replaced with fully charged batteries.

A TEAM EFFORT

TEAM WORK IS IMPORTANT FOR SOCCER, SCHOOL PROJECTS, AND ELECTRIC AIRPLANES. BATTERY CHEMISTS, AEROSPACE ENGINEERS, AND ELECTRIC VEHICLE EXPERTS WORK TOGETHER AT WRIGHT ELECTRIC. "WE NEED INPUT FROM LOTS OF PEOPLE," SAYS JEFFREY ENGLER. "THE PROJECT WON'T GET OFF THE GROUND UNLESS THE PEOPLE ON YOUR TEAM ARE VERY TALENTED."

CHAPTER FOUR

Airbus's electric aircraft prototypes, the Vahana and the CityAirbus, may replace taxis. The Vahana is designed to move passengers and cargo within a city. It features a passenger area nestled between two parallel wings. With four engines, it takes off and lands vertically, flying from building to building. The CityAirbus is a larger design that carries four passengers. Testing began in November 2017.

Until battery technology improves, many companies are developing hybrid planes. Zunum Aero and Boeing are building a plane that uses jet engines on takeoff and electric motors during flight. The plane carries battery packs in the wings and a small jet engine in the rear. By 2022, they aim to fly a plane that could carry 12 passengers up to 700 miles. "When you go in and do these things, they may not be immediately practical, but they all make an impression," says Ashish Kumar, Zunum Aero's founder. "And all those impressions eventually form a path."

Amazing Aircraft

As more companies race to successfully fly electric airplanes, their high-tech discoveries bring us a step closer to a greener world.

"Nothing of any fundamental and lasting value can be accomplished without trying things that have never been done before. Thanks to visionaries and pioneers, electric airplanes are not just an intriguing possibility. They are a reality."

—GEORGE BYE, BYE AEROSPACE

Fun Fact

Pilot training programs are using small two-seat electric planes with motors so light they can be held in two hands.

Chapter Five

THE FUTURE LOOKS ELECTRIC

Picture yourself taking an air taxi, hovering over crowded city streets. New prototypes could change city transportation. Electric air taxis would cut down on pollution and traffic. They could speed up travel times. Uber, a global taxi service company, aims to get a flying taxi service up and running before the 2028 Olympics in Los Angeles.

Within the next few years, small electric airplanes could be flying short routes. They would land at local airfields. "This is a market where the overwhelming majority of the journeys are now made by car, as it is not efficient to fly commercial," says Bar-Yohay of Eviation. "We are here to change this."

A TEAM AT NASA'S LANGLEY RESEARCH CENTER IS DEVELOPING A CONCEPT OF A BATTERY-POWERED PLANE THAT HAS 10 ENGINES AND CAN TAKE OFF LIKE A HELICOPTER AND FLY EFFICIENTLY LIKE AN AIRCRAFT. THE PROTOTYPE, CALLED GREASED LIGHTNING OR GL-10, IS CURRENTLY IN THE DESIGN AND TESTING PHASE. THE INITIAL THOUGHT WAS TO DEVELOP A 20-FOOT WINGSPAN (6.1 METERS) AIRCRAFT POWERED BY HYBRID DIESEL/ELECTRIC ENGINES, BUT THE TEAM STARTED WITH SMALLER VERSIONS FOR TESTING, BUILT BY RAPID PROTOTYPING.

CHAPTER FIVE

More personal aircraft may fill the skies in the near future. Using green technology, these small electric aircraft could offer advantages over cars. Teenagers might someday get a pilot's license instead of a driver's license.

In the future, the motors in electric airplanes will become more powerful. Electric airplanes will be capable of flying farther, faster, and carrying more weight. They could someday transport passengers and cargo around the world using clean, quiet technology.

The aviation industry faces big changes in the coming years. Airplanes dump tons of carbon dioxide into the air. The cost of jet fuel continues to rise. NASA predicts commercial passenger planes will be electric by 2035. "Aircraft and ships and all other forms of transport will go fully electric," says inventor Elon Musk. "Not half electric, but fully electric. No question." The first electric planes may be small, but they could transform the way people travel and pave the way to the future of aviation.

The Future Looks Electric

Fun Facts

1 The FlightPulse app shows pilots the amount of fuel used at different stages of a flight and how to reduce carbon emissions.

2 In 2016, a plane powered only by solar energy flew around the world.

Bertrand Piccard of Switzerland takes a selfie during the round-the-world trip with Solar Impulse 2 over the Arabian Peninsula in July 2016.

What You Should Know

- In 1903, the Wright Brothers flew the first airplane.

- The number of people traveling by airplane increases every year.

- When jet fuel burns, it releases carbon dioxide into the atmosphere, causing pollution.

- In 2016, NASA announced a plan to create a series of environmentally friendly airplanes.

- In 2017, many companies announced partnerships to develop electric airplanes.

Glossary

aerodynamic
The way air moves around an object

atmosphere
The layer of gases surrounding a planet

capacity
The amount that can be held by a container or space

composite
Made of various parts or materials

force
The push or pull upon an object

fossil fuel
Fuel formed over millions of years from the remains of plants and animals

hybrid
Using a combination of fuel and electricity

nonrenewable resource
A natural supply that cannot be replaced after it is used

prototype
The first model of a new machine or design

zero-emissions
Refers to an engine, motor, or process that does not produce harmful gas or pollution

Works Consulted

Adams, Eric. "The Age of Electric Aviation is Just 30 Years Away." *Wired*, May 31, 2017.

Bennet, Jay. "NASA's Next Great X-Plane Will Try to Revolutionize Electric Flight." *Popular Mechanics*, July 20, 2017.

Bye, George. "Cheaper, Lighter, Quieter: The Electrification of Flight is at Hand." *IEEE Spectrum*, August 22, 2017.

Gipson, Lillian. "Aeronautics Budget Proposes Return of X-Planes." *NASA*, February 18, 2016.

Jeffrey Engler, interview by author, February 2018.

Johnsson, Julie. "Boeing-Backed Startup Sees Hybrid-Electric Flights in Five Years." *Bloomberg*, October 5, 2017.

Mackersey, Ian. *The Wright Brothers*. London: Time Warner, 2004.

Miquel, Ros. "Future of Aviation." *CNN*, November 21, 2017.

Monaghan, Angela. "EasyJet Says It Could Be Flying Electric Planes Within a Decade." *Guardian*, September 27, 2017.

Thompson, Cadie. "Elon Musk Says He has a Design for an Electric Jet." *Business Insider*, October 15, 2015.

Further Reading

Kobasa, Paul, ed. *Green Transportation*. Chicago: World Book, Inc., 2010.

Old, Wendie, and Robert Parker. *To Fly: The Story of the Wright Brothers*. New York: Clarion Books, 2002.

Solway, Andrew. *Secrets of Flight*. New York: Marshall Cavendish Benchmark, 2011.

On the Internet

Smithsonian National Air and Space Museum
http://howthingsfly.si.edu

National Aeronautics and Space Administration
https://www.nasa.gov/audience/forstudents/index.html

The Earth Science Communications Team at NASA's Jet Propulsion Laboratory/California Institute of Technology
https://climatekids.nasa.gov

Index

aerodynamic   9, 19
Airbus   13, 22
Bar-Yohay, Omer   21, 24
batteries   8, 10, 16, 17, 18, 20, 21, 22
Boeing   7, 10, 22
Borer, Nick   15, 20
EasyJet   12, 13, 21
E Fan X   13
electric motors   8, 10, 13, 20, 22, 23, 26
Engler, Jeffrey   12, 21,
Eviation   10, 21, 24
forces   14
fossil fuel   6, 7

NASA
  X-57 (Maxwell)   10, 11, 15, 16, 20
  GL-10 (Greased Lightning)   25
pollution   6, 7, 8, 24, 28
prototypes   20, 24, 25
Wright Brothers   4, 5, 7, 8, 28
Wright Electric   12, 21
zero emissions   8
Zunum Aero   12, 22

About the Author

KERRILY SAPET is the author of 17 nonfiction books and many magazine articles for kids. This is her first book for Mitchell Lane Publishers. Researching and writing this book about greener aviation was interesting and inspiring as she is passionate about the environment and about taking care of the Earth. Kerrily currently lives in Illinois with her husband and two sons.